FOR BEN AND SAMMI

First published in the United States of America in January 2016 by Bloomsbury Children's Books
www.bloomsbury.com

Bloomsbury is a registered trademark of Bloomsbury Publishing Plc

For information about permission to reproduce selections from this book, write to
Permissions, Bloomsbury Children's Books, 1385 Broadway, New York, New York 10018
Bloomsbury books may be purchased for business or promotional use. For information on bulk purchases
please contact Macmillan Corporate and Premium Sales Department at specialmarkets@macmillan.com

Library of Congress Cataloging-in-Publication Data
Yoon, Salina, author, illustrator.
Be a friend / Salina Yoon.
pages   cm
Summary: Dennis is an ordinary boy who expresses himself in extraordinary ways. Some children do show-and-tell. Dennis mimes his.
Some children climb trees. Dennis is happy to BE a tree . . . But being a mime can be lonely. It isn't until Dennis meets a girl
named Joy that he discovers the power of friendship—and how special he truly is!
ISBN 978-1-61963-951-5 (hardcover) • ISBN 978-1-61963-952-2 (e-book) • ISBN 978-1-61963-953-9 (e-PDF)
[1. Individuality—Fiction. 2. Friendship—Fiction. 3. Pantomime—Fiction.] I. Title.
PZ7.Y817Be 2016   [E]—dc23   2015016227

Art created with pencil on paper and colored digitally • Typeset in Palatino and Rosewood Fill • Book design by Salina Yoon and Donna Mark
Printed in China by Leo Paper Products, Heshan, Guangdong
3 5 7 9 10 8 6 4 2

All papers used by Bloomsbury Publishing, Inc., are natural, recyclable products made from wood grown in well-managed
forests. The manufacturing processes conform to the environmental regulations of the country of origin.

BE A FRIEND

SALINA YOON

BLOOMSBURY

NEW YORK   LONDON   OXFORD   NEW DELHI   SYDNEY

DENNIS was an

ordinary boy . . .

. . . who expressed himself in **EXTRAORDINARY** ways.

Everyone called him

MIME BOY.

Dennis didn't speak a word.

He would only **ACT**—in scenes.

Some children would SHOW and TELL in class.

Dennis would **MIME** instead.

EGG

CATERPILLAR

CHRYSALIS

BUTTERFLY

Some children liked to **CLIMB** a tree.

Dennis was happy to **BE** a tree.

But even trees get **LONELY** sometimes.

Dennis felt INVISIBLE.

It was as if he were standing on the other side of a **WALL**.

Until . . .

One day Dennis kicked an **IMAGINARY** ball . . .

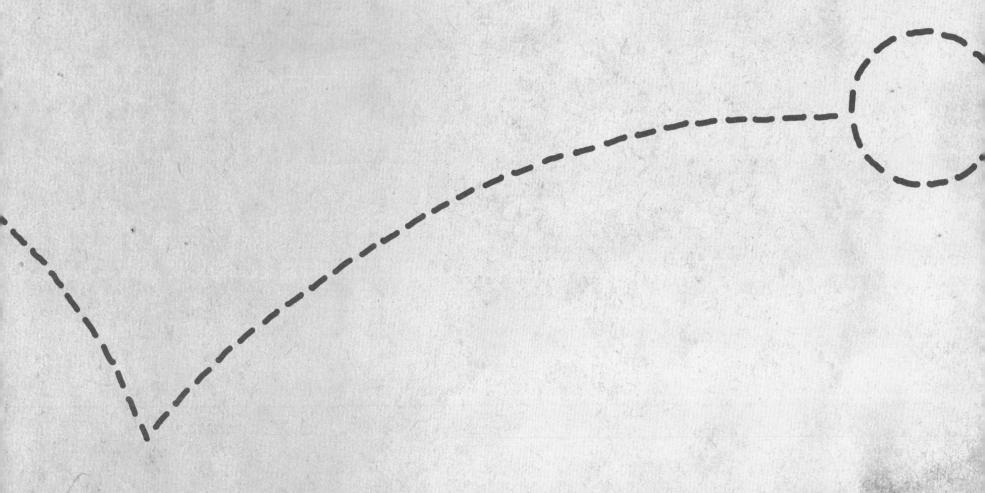

. . . and someone **CAUGHT** it!

Her name was **JOY**.

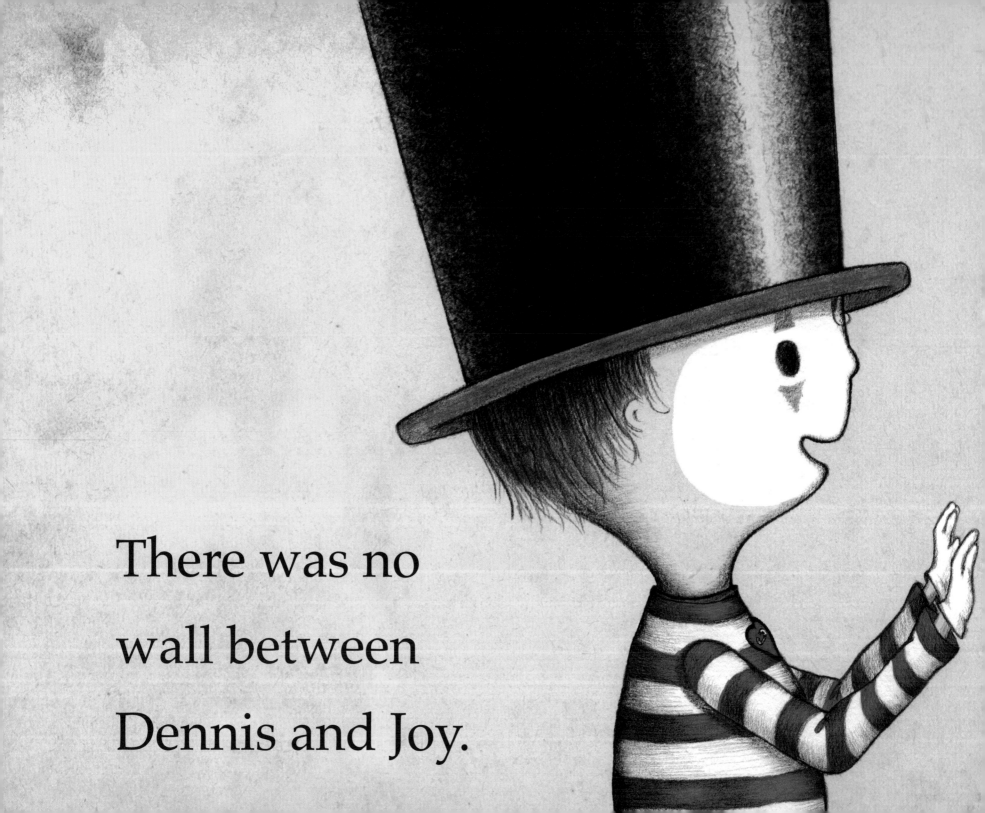

There was no
wall between
Dennis and Joy.

It was more

like a **MIRROR**.

They saw the world the **SAME** way.

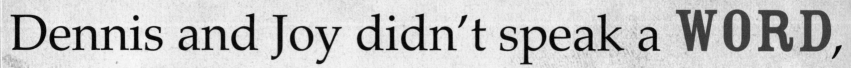

Dennis and Joy didn't speak a **WORD,**

because **FRIENDS** don't have to.

But they laughed out loud with
JAZZ HANDS...

. . . for all the world to **SEE**!